Text and illustrations © Céline Leopold 1973 ISBN 0 370 01129 5
Printed in Great Britain for The Bodley Head Ltd,
9 Bow Street, London WC2E 7AL
by William Clowes & Sons Ltd, Beccles
First published 1973

BABA YAGA

A picture book by
CÉLINE LEOPOLD

THE BODLEY HEAD
London Sydney Toronto

Once upon a time, far far away, in dense and dark woods, there lived a terrible witch called Baba Yaga. Her hut stood on two giant chicken legs and was surrounded by human bones and skulls with a flame burning inside each one.

Baba Yaga had teeth made of iron which she would sharpen with a big rusty file while she thought about the naughty children she would eat for supper the next day.

When she went out Baba Yaga travelled in a mortar, a huge bowl that made a terrible noise. In her hands she carried the pestle; behind her a broom, guided by invisible hands, swept away all traces of her journey.

In a nearby village there lived a young girl whose name was Wassilisa the Beautiful. Since the death of her mother Wassilisa had lived alone with her father but he was a merchant and was often away. Before she died Wassilisa's mother had given her daughter a doll saying, "Take special care of this doll, my child. Share your food with it and it will talk to you and help you in time of distress. But be sure never to show the doll to another soul."

After some years Wassilisa's father married again and his new wife was a widow with two daughters of the same age as his own child.

The stepmother was jealous of Wassilisa and of her father's love for her and she made the girl do all the work in the house. Wassilisa toiled all day but still she remained as fresh as ever and her stepmother was very angry. She did not know that the magic doll was helping Wassilisa.

One night, when Wassilisa's father was away on a long journey, the wicked stepmother resolved to get rid of Wassilisa. The woman and her daughters were sitting sewing by the light of a candle and, seeing her chance, the woman threw open a window and a strong gust of wind blew out the candle.

"Wassilisa," she called, "our light has blown out. You must go to Baba Yaga's hut in the woods and fetch us some fire so we can light the candle again." Wassilisa was very frightened for the night was as black as pitch but before she set out she went to her room to tell her magic doll.

"Take me with you in your pocket," said the doll. "I will keep you safe." As they left the house Wassilisa heard the wicked stepmother laughing and telling her daughters that the girl would never return.

Blinded by her tears and confused by the dark Wassilisa was soon lost in the forest. She reached into her pocket and took out her doll and together they sat by a tree stump. "Please help me, little doll," she pleaded. At that moment Wassilisa heard the sound of horse's hooves and through the trees rode a horseman clothed all in red. As he passed the night became lighter with a rosy glow as if the dawn were breaking.

Wassilisa could now see the path before her and she continued her journey with the doll safely tucked in her pocket.

Not long afterwards there came the sound of horse's hooves for the second time and a horseman clothed all in white passed through the trees. Behind him came the daylight and there in front of Wassilisa was Baba Yaga's hut.

Wassilisa was terrified and as she stood before the hut she heard the sound of horse's hooves for the third time and through the trees came a horseman clothed all in black. At once night fell upon the forest again. Then a great thundering filled the air and a shrill voice screamed out, "I smell strangers. Who is here?" And out of the night came Baba Yaga riding in her mortar.

"My name is Wassilisa and I've been sent to fetch some fire." Wassilisa trembled.

"Some fire—eh?" screamed the witch, cackling with laughter. "You will have to work for your fire, my child. And if you fail to please me I shall eat you for my supper," and she pushed Wassilisa before her into the hut.

"Fetch me all the food in the house," demanded Baba Yaga and Wassilisa fetched and carried until the table was covered with enough food for ten hungry men. Then the witch called for a large pitcher of wine and a barrel of beer and she sat down to eat and drink her fill. When she was satisfied she handed Wassilisa a crust of bread and a morsel of meat.

"Take your supper," she said. "Eat well, for tomorrow there is work to do. You will clean the hut and cook my meals but your main task will be to separate every grain in this sack of corn. You must put the good seeds into one pile and the bad ones in another. If you have not finished the task by the time I return at nightfall I will eat you for my supper." So saying the witch lay down and went to sleep. The hut trembled from top to bottom with the sound of her snoring.

Poor Wassilisa cried herself to sleep that night as she lay holding her doll close to her.

Early the next morning as Baba Yaga flew off in her mortar, Wassilisa gave her doll some of the bread saved from her meagre supper and pleaded for help.

"Do not worry, dear Wassilisa," said the doll. "Your task is already done. All that is left to do is to prepare Baba Yaga's supper." And Wassilisa saw that the grain was indeed separated.

When Baba Yaga returned she was very angry that everything had been done and vowed to give Wassilisa a more difficult task the following day. "Tomorrow," she said, "you must spin a single thread, unbroken, from the wool in this sack." So saying she lay down and went to sleep and the hut trembled from top to bottom with the sound of her snoring.

The next morning when Baba Yaga had flown away, Wassilisa again took out her precious doll. "Do not worry, dear Wassilisa," said the doll. "Your task is already done. The wool is spun into a single thread." And Wassilisa saw that it was unbroken.

When Baba Yaga returned she was very angry. "Tomorrow," she said, "you must fill the big tub with water using only a sieve." But Wassilisa was no longer frightened for she knew that her doll would help her.

In the morning, almost before the sound of Baba Yaga's mortar had died away, the tub was full.

In the evening, as Wassilisa looked to see if Baba Yaga was coming, she saw the black-robed horseman riding past and behind him the day turned into night—and Baba Yaga thundered back to the hut.

"What are you doing at the window, child?" she screamed.

"I was looking for you, Baba Yaga, but saw only a dark horseman riding through the trees."

"That was Night," said the witch quickly. "There are three riders who pass this way, Night, Dawn and Day, all my servants. But if you'll mind your business, I'll mind mine." And when she saw that the tub was full she was very angry and vowed to set Wassilisa an impossible task on the next day. So saying she lay down and slept, and the hut trembled with her snoring.

Wassilisa ran to her doll. "We must leave at once," said the doll. "Bring this comb and cloth with you and take one of the lighted skulls to show us the path."

Putting the doll safely in her pocket, Wassilisa did as she was bid and ran from the hut.

Just then Wassilisa heard a dreadful rumbling sound and she knew at once that Baba Yaga had woken and was coming after her.

"Quickly, throw down the cloth," called the doll from her pocket.

As it hit the ground the cloth became a roaring racing river and there was Baba Yaga dancing and screaming with rage on the far bank—for, as you know, witches cannot fly over water.

Wassilisa turned and ran deeper into the forest, for she knew that it would not be long before Baba Yaga would find a way to cross the river.

On and on she ran. The hard ground hurt her feet and far away behind her she heard the dreadful rumbling sound again. Baba Yaga's mortar and pestle were bumping and shaking the ground and getting nearer every minute.

"Quickly, throw down the comb," came the faint voice from inside Wassilisa's pocket.

As it hit the ground the comb became a vast and thorny thicket and Baba Yaga danced and screamed with rage as the thorns closed over her head. Her way was barred.

Wassilisa ran and ran and suddenly she was at the edge of the forest and her father's cottage was before her.

The wicked stepmother and her daughters were shocked to see Wassilisa return but before they had time to speak the skull in Wassilisa's hand leapt at them, shooting flames from its eyes. The three of them fled into the forest screaming and were never seen again.

At that moment Wassilisa's father returned to the cottage from his long journey. When he heard the dreadful tale that his daughter had to tell, he gathered her in his arms and promised never to leave her again. So the two of them lived happily ever after and Wassilisa never forgot that it was her precious little doll that had saved her from the wicked Baba Yaga.